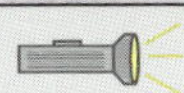

Tools Search Notes Discuss Go!

CANADA

A MyReportLinks.com Book

PAT McCARTHY

MyReportLinks.com Books
an imprint of

Enslow Publishers, Inc.

Box 398, 40 Industrial Road
Berkeley Heights, NJ 07922
USA

MyReportLinks.com Books, an imprint of Enslow Publishers, Inc. MyReportLinks®
is a registered trademark of Enslow Publishers, Inc.

Library of Congress Cataloging-in-Publication Data

McCarthy, Pat, 1940–
Canada / Pat McCarthy.
v. cm. — (Top ten countries of recent immigrants)
Includes bibliographical references and index.
Contents: Canada: an overview — Land and climate — Culture — Economy
— History — Canadian immigrants' place in America.
ISBN 0-7660-5176-5
1. Canada—Juvenile literature. [1. Canada. 2. Canadian Americans.]
I. Title. II. Series.
F1008.2.M34 2004
971—dc22

2003015242

Printed in the United States of America

10 9 8 7 6 5 4 3 2 1

To Our Readers:
Through the purchase of this book, you and your library gain access to the Report Links that specifically back up this book.
The Publisher will provide access to the Report Links that back up this book and will keep these Report Links up to date on **www.myreportlinks.com** for three years from the book's first publication date.
We have done our best to make sure all Internet addresses in this book were active and appropriate when we went to press. However, the author and the Publisher have no control over, and assume no liability for, the material available on those Internet sites or on other Web sites they may link to.
The usage of the MyReportLinks.com Books Web site is subject to the terms and conditions stated on the Usage Policy Statement on **www.myreportlinks.com**.
A password may be required to access the Report Links that back up this book. The password is found on the bottom of page 4 of this book.
Any comments or suggestions can be sent by e-mail to comments@myreportlinks.com or to the address on the back cover.

Photo Credits: © Corel Corporation, pp. 1, 9, 11, 13, 14, 19, 20, 23, 24, 30, 34, 42; Artville, p. 3; Canadian Museum of Civilization, pp. 26, 32, 36; Enslow Publishers, Inc., p. 17; Library of Congress, p. 37; MyReportLinks.com Books, p. 4, back cover; National Archives of Canada, pp. 25, 40; National Library of Canada, p. 39; Robert Carlone, p. 1; *The World Factbook 2003*, pp. 1, 9 (flags).

Cover Photo: Inuit girl, Lake Louise, © Corel Corporation; boy fishing, Robert Carlone; *The World Factbook 2003* (flags).

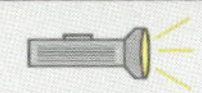

Tools Search Notes Discuss Go!

Contents

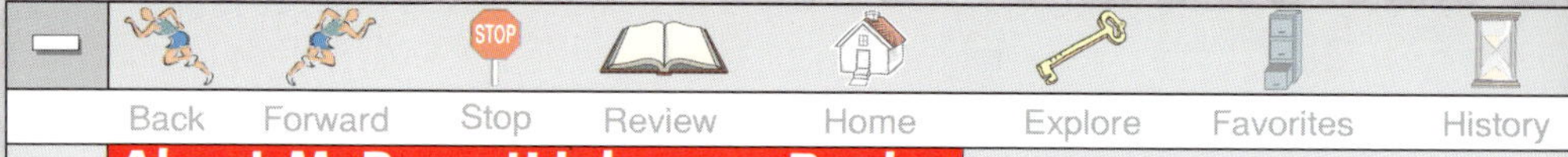

MyReportLinks.com Books

Great Books, Great Links, Great for Research!

The Report Links listed on the following four pages can save you hours of research time by **instantly** bringing you to the best Web sites relating to your report topic.

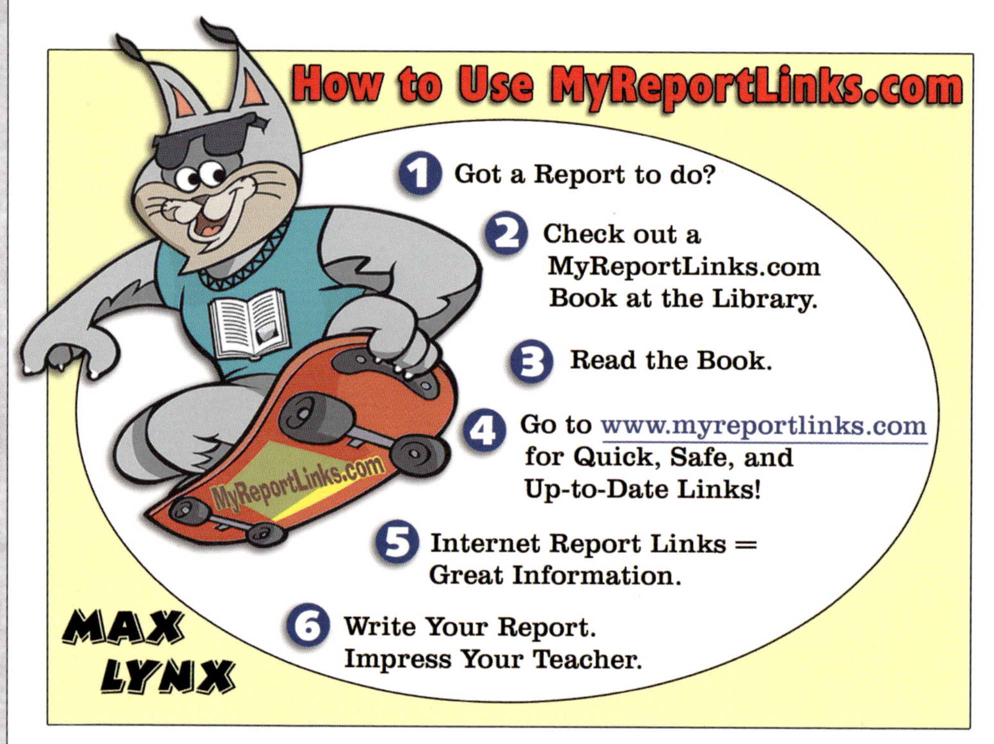

The pre-evaluated Web sites are your links to source documents, photographs, illustrations, and maps. They also provide links to dozens—even hundreds—of Web sites about your report subject.

MyReportLinks.com Books and the MyReportLinks.com Web site save you time and make report writing easier than ever!

Please see "To Our Readers" on the copyright page for important information about this book, the MyReportLinks.com Web site, and the Report Links that back up this book. Please enter **ICA7862** if asked for a password.

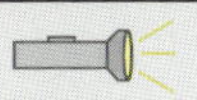

Report Links

The Internet sites described below can be accessed at http://www.myreportlinks.com

*EDITOR'S CHOICE

▶ The *World Factbook*: Canada

This page from the *World Factbook* contains statistics about Canada. Geography, people, government, economy, communications, and more are covered in this site.

*EDITOR'S CHOICE

▶ Civilization.ca

This site created by the Canadian Museum of Civilization provides information on archaeology, arts and crafts, cultures, civilizations, exhibitions, and military history.

*EDITOR'S CHOICE

▶ National Archives of Canada

The Web site of the National Archives of Canada includes photographs and writings of the important people, places, and events in Canadian history.

*EDITOR'S CHOICE

▶ Great Canadian Parks

Learn about Canada's national parks from this site. Information on each park's ecology, history, and culture is included.

*EDITOR'S CHOICE

▶ Canada Site

This official site of the government of Canada provides up-to-date information on Canadian government offices, agencies, news, land, climate, economy, history, services, and jobs.

*EDITOR'S CHOICE

▶ Canadian Embassy, Washington, D.C.

The official Web site of the Canadian Embassy in Washington, D.C., includes information on the economy, government, and culture of Canada, and discusses the relationship between Canada and the United States.

The Internet sites described below can be accessed at http://www.myreportlinks.com

About Ottawa

This is the official Web site for the city of Ottawa, the capital of Canada. There is a brief history of the city as well as a listing of attractions and important places.

Alcan Highway

The Alcan (Alaskan-Canadian) Highway between Dawson Creek, British Columbia, and Fairbanks, Alaska, runs for 1,522 miles. This site includes a history and images of the road's construction.

By Way of Canada

This article from the United States National Archives and Records Administration contains information on the history of immigrants coming to the United States via Canada.

Canada's Land and People

This site provides information on Canadian geography. Maps, photos, and additional resources are included.

Canadian Charter of Rights and Freedoms

This site contains information on the Canadian Charter of Rights and Freedoms, which is part of the Canadian Constitution, and discusses the rights and freedoms that Canadians are entitled to as citizens.

Canadian Heroes in Fact and Fiction: Louis Riel

On this site, you will find a brief biography of Louis Riel, a Métis leader who fought for his people's rights in the nineteenth century.

The Canadian Literature Archive

The Canadian Literature Archive provides information on Canadian authors. Included are bibliographies, author profiles, photos, events, and links to other sites.

Canadian Pacific Railway

The image gallery contains photos and graphic art from the Canadian Pacific Railway Archives covering the history of Canada and the railroad. There is also a brief history and links to related sites.

Report Links

The Internet sites described below can be accessed at http://www.myreportlinks.com

CN Tower: Canada's Wonder of the World

At 1,815 feet (553 meters), the CN Tower in Toronto, Ontario, is the tallest building in the world. The tower's site includes a virtual tour of the building, lists its many attractions, and offers views that can be had from its observation deck.

Confederation for Kids

This site from the National Library of Canada discusses Canada's history from its colonial days to the present.

Economy Overview

The site from the Canadian government provides a basic overview of Canada's economy.

Expo 67—Montreal World's Fair

This site provides photos and information on Expo 67, the World's Fair that was held in Montreal, Quebec. Click on "Maps" to get a view of the entire area and to view photos of individual sites and attractions.

Get 2 Know Canada

This site provides facts and statistics about Canada. There is also a link to the Web site of the prime minister of Canada.

The Glenn Gould Archive

The National Library of Canada has a site containing the archives of Glenn Gould, a Canadian pianist. You can read a biography of his life and listen to recordings of his music.

History: Greatness Personified

This site provides an in-depth look at the hockey career of Wayne Gretzky, the most prolific scorer in NHL history and one of the most popular athletes in Canada.

History Lands

This site provides information on many of Canada's most important historical sites and offers a virtual tour of those places.

The Internet sites described below can be accessed at http://www.myreportlinks.com

The History of Canada

This site offers a history of Canada, from earliest times to the present.

Jacques Cartier: Navigator-Explorer

This site provides an in-depth look into the life and adventures of Jacques Cartier, the French navigator and explorer who was the first European to see the St. Lawrence River.

Meteorological Service of Canada (MSC)

On the Meteorological Service of Canada site, you will find current conditions and local forecasts as well as interesting weather facts and trivia. There are also links to past weather-related events.

The Métis Nation of Ontario

This Métis Nation of Ontario site provides information on the Métis people of that province and includes information on their culture, communities, language, arts, businesses, news, and events.

Royal Canadian Mounted Police

The Royal Canadian Mounted Police, popularly known as the Mounties, are Canada's national police force. Their Web site includes RCMP history as well as information about their organization and practices.

TSN.ca

This site from Canada's all-sports network, which includes statistics and is updated daily, provides news on Canadian and American sports from a Canadian perspective.

Welcome to Inuit Tapiriit Kanatami

This Inuit Tapiriit Kanatami organization site provides information on the history of the Inuit people in Canada. It also includes information on current issues that are important to the Inuit.

The Work of Arthur Erickson

On this site you can read a brief biography of Arthur Erickson, an influential Canadian architect. You can also view photos of some of his designs.

Canada Facts

Capital
Ottawa

Population
32,207,113 (July 2003 estimate)

Total Area
3,851,788 square miles (9,976,140 square kilometers), the second largest country in the world, behind Russia.

Water Area
291,571 square feet (755,170 square kilometers)

Highest Point
Mount Logan, 19,551 feet (5,959 meters)

Lowest Point
Sea level along the Atlantic coastline

Location
Northern North America

Type of Government
Confederation with parliamentary democracy

Sovereign
Queen Elizabeth II

Monetary Unit
Canadian dollar

Languages
English, French, and native languages.

Religions
Roman Catholic 46%, Protestant 36%, other 18%

National Anthem
"O, Canada"

Flag
The flag has a wide red vertical bar on each side of a white field containing an eleven-pointed red maple leaf.

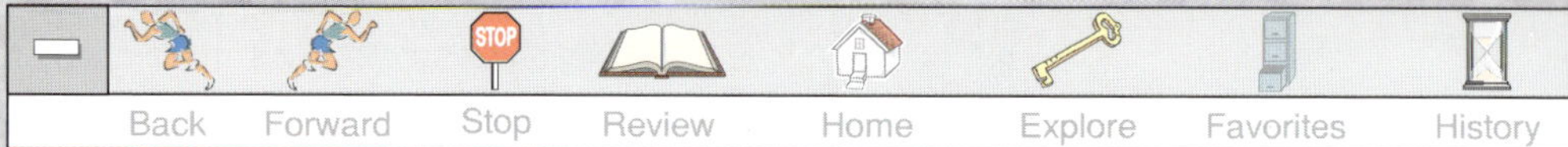

Chapter 1

Canada: Land of Beauty and Resources

Canada, the second largest country in the world in area, extends from the Pacific Ocean to the Atlantic Ocean on the North American continent. It is bordered by the Arctic Ocean to the north and the United States to the south. Like its southern neighbor, Canada is a blend of cultures, including English, French, and native cultures. Canada and the United States also share the world's longest undefended border, and Canada's relationship with the United States has long been one of friendliness and peace. That peace has not always been without uneasiness, however. As former Canadian prime minister Pierre Trudeau once told an American audience, "Living next to you is in some ways like sleeping with an elephant. No matter how friendly or even-tempered the beast, if I may call it that, one is affected by every twitch and grunt."[1]

Expansive Beauty

Canada is richly endowed with natural resources, including fertile farmland, trees for lumber and papermaking, and many minerals. Canada is also a land of great natural beauty—a land of lofty snow-covered mountains, wide fertile plains, wild rocky coastlines, and numerous lakes, rivers, and islands. A number of national parks and other places preserve this beauty for all to enjoy.

At Banff and Jasper National Parks, people are awed by the spectacular mountain scenery of the Canadian Rockies. Fundy National Park is home to the highest tides

The view looking north along the Rocky Mountain Trench at Peyto Lake, set in a deep glacial valley of Banff National Park.

in the world. Cape Breton Highlands National Park offers wonderful views of the rocky Atlantic coastline. Niagara Falls is a scenic wonder shared by Canada and the United States. The falls are located in the Niagara River, between the two countries.

Canada's Government

Canada's government is a confederation with a parliamentary democracy. A confederation is a group of countries or provinces joined together for the purpose of defense and government.

Queen Elizabeth II of Great Britain is head of state for Canada, but she does not rule the nation. She serves as a symbol of the traditional British customs and laws. She

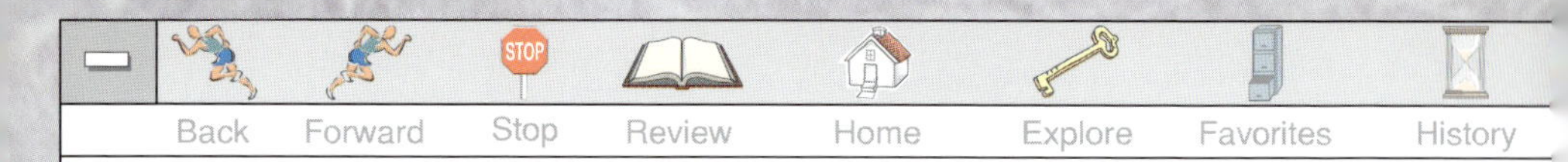

is represented in Canada's government by Governor General Adrienne Clarkson. The actual head of government in Canada is the prime minister. In December 2003, Paul Martin was inaugurated Canada's twenty-first prime minister, succeeding Jean Chrétien.

Canada's legislature is made up of two houses, the Senate and the House of Commons. Senators are nominated by the prime minister and appointed by the governor general. Members of the House of Commons are elected by the voters.

Provinces and Territories

Canada is made up of ten provinces (like states) and three territories. The eastern provinces, sometimes known as the Atlantic Provinces, are New Brunswick, Newfoundland and Labrador, Nova Scotia, and Prince Edward Island.

West of these provinces are Quebec, where French culture and language dominate, and Ontario, the most populated of the provinces. Farther west are Manitoba, Saskatchewan, and Alberta, sometimes called the Prairie Provinces.

Bordering the Pacific Ocean is British Columbia. North of the western and central provinces are the Yukon Territory, the Northwest Territories, and Nunavut, which was once the eastern part of the Northwest Territories. It was made a separate territory on April 1, 1999.

Canada's Cities

Ottawa, Ontario, a city of just over a million people, is the capital of Canada and the seat of government. Parliament Hill is the site of the federal government buildings. Ottawa is also home to the National Gallery of Canada, which houses the world's largest collection of Canadian art.

Montreal, Quebec, founded in 1642 by a handful of French settlers, is today the largest French-speaking city in North America. One of the most festive areas in Montreal is Place Jacques-Cartier, a colorful marketplace filled with vendors, performers, and horse-drawn carriages. The city is also home to the legendary National Hockey League Montreal Canadiens as well as the Montreal Expos major league baseball team.

Toronto, on Lake Ontario, is Canada's largest city, with more than 4 million people, and is the country's financial center. The Toronto skyline is dominated by the famous 1,815-foot CN Tower, nicknamed "Canada's Wonder of the World," which offers breathtaking views for miles around. A communications tower that houses many offices, the tower also features an arcade where visitors can ride a famous aircraft, fight a wildfire, or undertake a dangerous mission, all through simulated

The view of Toronto's skyline features the SkyDome, to the left, next to the CN Tower.

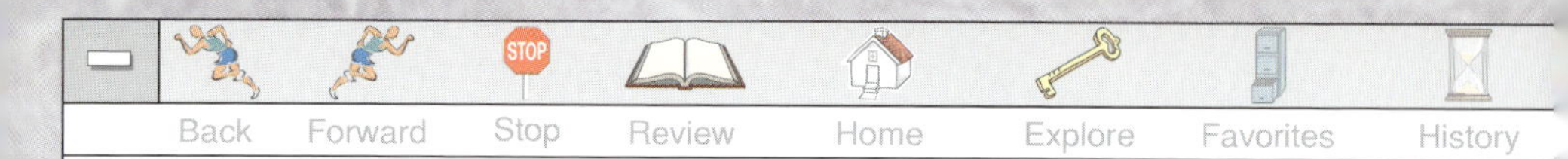

A stroll through this neighborhood in the Old Town in Quebec City reminds one of the city's French past and French-Canadian present.

games. The Toronto Blue Jays play baseball in the SkyDome, and the Toronto Maple Leafs play hockey and the Toronto Raptors play basketball at the Air Canada Centre.

Vancouver, surrounded by water on three sides, is the third largest city in Canada. Known for its spectacular views of the ocean and mountains, it has one of the mildest climates in Canada, and it is home to more than 190 parks.

Some other notable Canadian cities include Quebec City, which like Montreal, is predominantly French-speaking and is filled with Old World charm, and Calgary, Alberta, home to the famous Calgary Stampede.

Famous Canadians

Canada is the birthplace of many people who have achieved fame in the fields of art and entertainment. Celine Dion, the popular singer, was born just outside Montreal, Quebec, into a musical family, and she began singing with her sisters and brothers when she was five. Shania Twain, born in Ontario, has found fame in the field of country music. Other singers who hail from Canada include Joni Mitchell, Buffy Sainte-Marie, Gordon Lightfoot, and Neil Young.

Famous Canadian writers include Lucy Maud Montgomery, the author of *Anne of Green Gables*, and Margaret Atwood, of Toronto, famous for her novels that deal with relationships and modern life. Robertson Davies, W. P. Kinsella, and Mordecai Richler are Canadian novelists whose works have won wide acclaim.

Comedians and actors who were born in Canada but have gone on to find fame in American movies and television include Michael J. Fox, Dan Aykroyd, Martin Short, Mike Myers, and Norm Macdonald.

In the world of sports, there is perhaps no better-known Canadian than Wayne Gretzky, considered one of the greatest hockey players of all time. He is the all-time scoring leader in the NHL. Nicknamed "The Great One," Gretzky now manages Canada's Olympic hockey team.

Chapter 2

Land and Climate

Canada has a wide variety of landforms and climates. This nearly 4-million-square-mile country is made up of six geographic regions. These are the Cordillera, the Interior Plains, the Canadian Shield, the Great Lakes-St. Lawrence Lowlands, the Appalachian region, and the Arctic region.

The Cordillera

The far western mountainous region bordering the Pacific Ocean is the Cordillera. It runs through the provinces of British Columbia and western Alberta and part of the Yukon Territory. The breathtakingly beautiful Canadian Rockies are here as are lowlands, valleys, and plateaus.

Most people in this region live in the southern lowlands and on the plateaus, where the climate is more temperate. This part of Canada also has active volcanoes, and earthquakes do occur there.

Interior Plains

East of the Cordillera are the Interior Plains, also called the Prairies. The plains cover eastern Alberta and all of Saskatchewan and Manitoba. This region is one of the greatest grain-producing regions in the world. Livestock, including cattle, pigs, and poultry, are also raised here. The scenery is not as spectacular as that in the Cordillera, but the wide expanses of golden grain have a beauty of their own.

Canadian Shield

The Canadian Shield surrounds the gigantic Hudson Bay in central Canada. This rocky region has only a thin layer of soil covering the rock. The soil was scraped off by advancing and retreating glaciers. There is enough soil to support forests of spruce, fir, pine, and tamarack trees. Buried in the rock are minerals such as gold, silver, copper, zinc, and uranium. Most of Canada's mining towns are located within the Canadian Shield.

A map of Canada.

Great Lakes-St. Lawrence Lowlands

The Great Lakes-St. Lawrence Lowlands region includes Ontario and southern Quebec. This is the most populated region of Canada, and most of the country's manufacturing is found here.[1] The land surrounding the Great Lakes is fertile farmland, ideal for growing grapes, peaches, pears, and other fruits. Many sugar maple trees grow in this region, and the sap is collected every spring to make maple syrup and maple sugar.

Appalachian Region

The Appalachian region is home to Canada's Atlantic or Maritime Provinces: New Brunswick, Nova Scotia, Prince Edward Island, and Newfoundland and Labrador all have shorelines on the Atlantic Ocean. These were the first provinces to be settled by Europeans. The Grand Banks, a shallow continental shelf extending hundreds of miles off the coast of Newfoundland, was once one of the richest fishing grounds in the world, but overfishing, especially of cod, has led to much-depleted stocks.

The coast provides spectacular views of the ocean with its rocky shores and pounding waves. Farther inland, the land is covered with low, rugged hills and plateaus, what is left of the ancient Appalachian Mountain range. The mountains here are lower than those in the west. The fertile soil is good for farming, important to the region's economy.

Arctic Region

The northernmost part of Canada is the Arctic region. This land lies north of the tree line, the point at which trees can no longer grow. It is light almost twenty-four hours a day in summer, but in winter, sunlight is somewhat scarce.

A fishing village in Newfoundland. Despite the quaint charm captured in this photo, fishermen in the Maritimes face difficult weather conditions and uncertain futures.

Most of the area is tundra, a vast treeless plain. Plants grow very slowly, and the ground is fragile. The region is still the least populated of any in Canada. Some of the people living in the Arctic work in the oil industry, but most of the residents are Inuit and First Nations peoples. They live mainly by fishing and hunting, as their ancestors did for centuries, although some now use snowmobiles for transportation instead of the more-traditional dogsleds.

Rivers and Lakes

There are many lakes in Canada, but the Great Lakes deserve special mention. Lake Ontario, Lake Erie, Lake Michigan, Lake Superior, and Lake Huron, which lie between Canada and the United States, are important for shipping, trade, transportation, and recreation. The system

Ottawa's winter temperatures make for great outdoor skating, like this jaunt along the Rideau Canal.

of lakes and rivers in the Great Lakes region that was used by early explorers and fur traders in Canada has evolved into the St. Lawrence Seaway system. It enables goods and people to travel from ports on any of the Great Lakes through the St. Lawrence River and to the Atlantic.

The St. Lawrence is just one of Canada's important rivers. Others include the Fraser River in British Columbia, the Peace River in Alberta, the Churchill River, which runs through Saskatchewan and Manitoba, and the Nelson River in Manitoba.

A Varied Climate

Canada's climate varies greatly from region to region and is affected by the country's varied landforms.

The mildest climate is found in the Cordillera, where the coast is shielded from storms by Vancouver Island. Most of the area receives little snowfall except in the mountains. The valleys have hot summers and little rain.

The Interior Plains have cold winters and hot, humid summers.

The Canadian Shield has long, cold winters with lots of snow. Temperatures vary greatly within this huge region.

The Great Lakes-St. Lawrence region has snowy, windy winters and fairly long and humid summers.

The Atlantic Provinces are noted for their variable climate. Winters bring a good deal of snow, and fog is common in spring and summer.

The Arctic region is snow covered most of the year and has permafrost, a permanently frozen layer below the surface of the earth. Only a few inches of the top layer thaw during the short two-month summer. Temperatures are above freezing for only a few weeks a year.

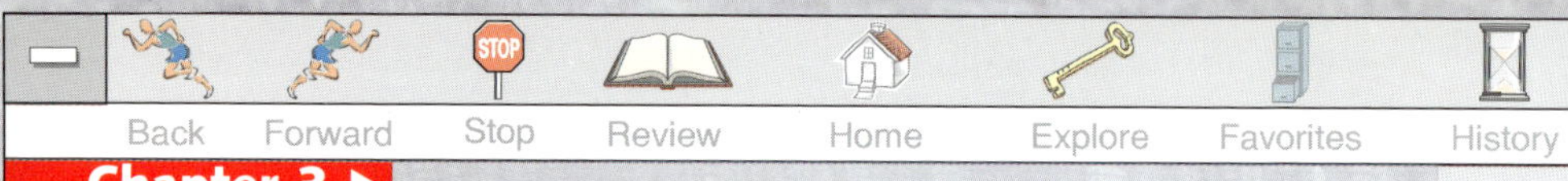

Chapter 3

Culture

Canada's culture has been influenced by French and English settlers as well as by aboriginal peoples whose ancestors were the land's original inhabitants. Canada's immigration policies have also led to many people from other countries settling in Canada.

About a million Canadians have some aboriginal blood. That is, they are the descendants of the original people of North America. About one fourth of these people speak an aboriginal language.[1] Canada's aboriginal people are divided into three groups—the Inuit, the First Nations, and the Métis. There is even a national holiday in Canada observed on June 21 called National Aboriginal Day, which celebrates the customs, culture, and contributions of these three groups.

The Inuit

The Canadian Inuit live in four Inuit regions of Canada: Inuvialuit, which is part of the Northwest Territories; Nunavit; Nunavik, in northern Quebec; and northern Labrador. The name *Inuit* means "people" in their language, Inuktitut. About 55,700 Inuit live in Canada, and their population has increased rapidly over the past few decades.[2]

Those living on the northern coast learned to hunt marine animals in winter when ice covered everything on the land. They became expert at hunting seals, walruses, whales, and caribou.

Inuit artists today keep their culture alive by making beautiful sculptures and carvings from bone, ivory, antlers, and wood. They also fashion art from soapstone, a soft rock that they carve into interesting objects.

First Nations

The many North American Indian tribes of Canada are collectively known as the First Nations. They speak more than fifty different languages and dialects. Over 70 percent of them live on reservations, land set aside for them by the government.[3]

Like the Inuit, the First Nations people probably arrived in Canada from Asia. They first saw Europeans when the Vikings visited Newfoundland around A.D. 1000. Later settlements arrived from France and England.

In 1830, the British in Canada instituted a new policy to force First Nations tribes onto reservations, while their land was sold to settlers.

An Inuit fisherman in Canada's Northwest Territories.

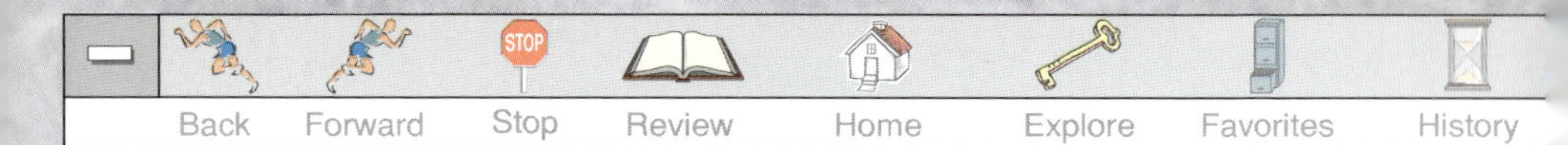

These intricately carved and beautifully colored totems, identifying families or clans, are First Nations works of art in Vancouver's Stanley Park.

The government expected the First Nations people to live in houses, farm the land, and be educated by the missionaries, who tried to convert them to Christianity. The land on these reservations was divided among First Nations tribes, who resisted such division because they did not believe in individual people or groups owning land.

Canada became a confederation in 1867, and soon after, the Canadian Parliament tried to turn the reservations into towns and outlawed many traditional practices. It also imposed a male-dominated culture on the First Nations tribes, many of which had been governed by women.

The First Nations people of Canada, like their American Indian counterparts, resented the intervention of government. They developed organizations across Canada to assert their rights and preserve their culture. Canada's First Nations people have become more powerful in politics over the years. They have even taken their cause to the United Nations in an effort to retain their rights, livelihoods, and identity.

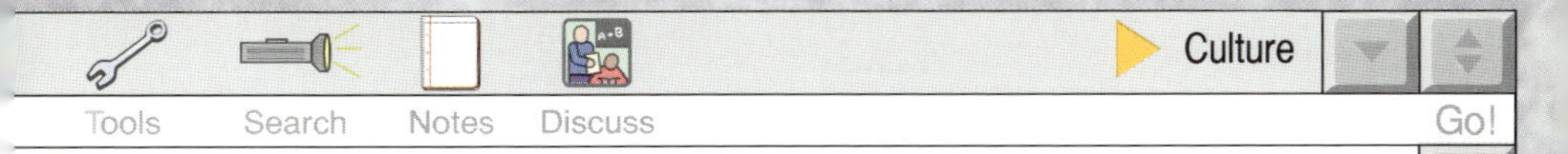

The Métis

Métis are Canadians who are of mixed native and European background. The original Métis had native mothers and European fathers. The Métis call themselves "The Forgotten People." They have often been ignored or looked down on by both the First Nations and nonaboriginal Canadians.

During the last half of the nineteenth century, the Métis demanded representation in Parliament, an elected legislature, and other considerations. The Manitoba Act of 1870 granted some of their requests. It gave them over

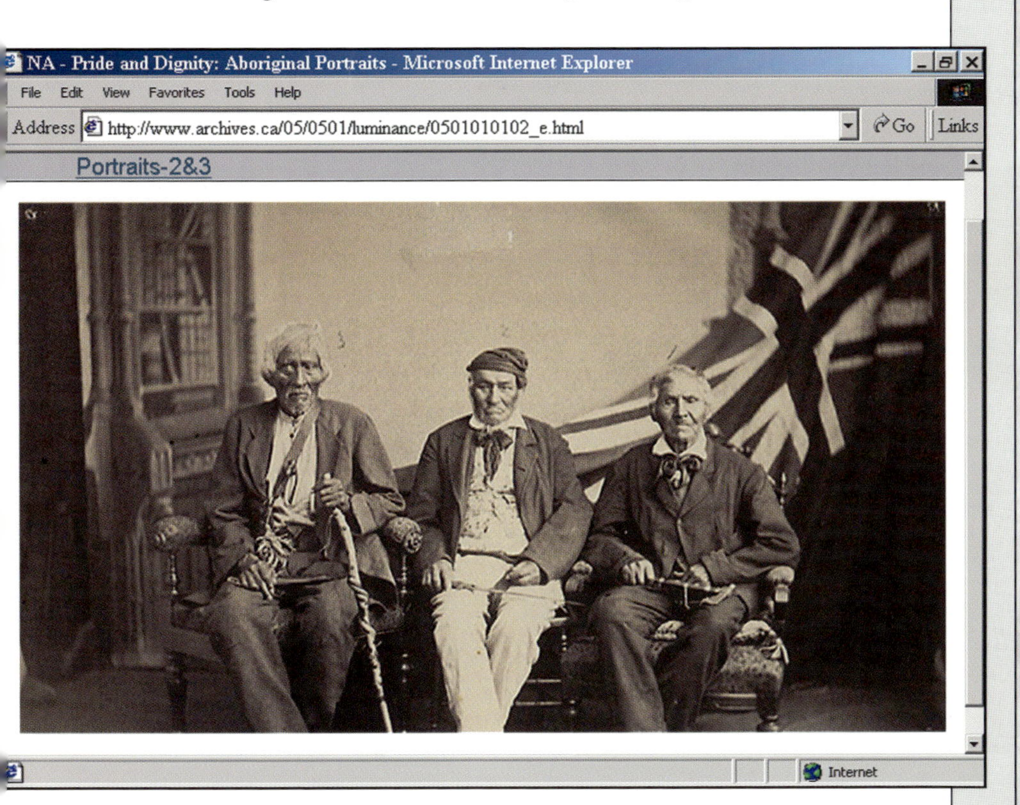

This 1882 portrait shows the three remaining Six Nations warriors who fought with the British in the War of 1812. The Six Nations, also known as the Iroquois Confederacy, were the Mohawk, Oneida, Onondaga, Cayuga, and Seneca, and later the Tuscarora.

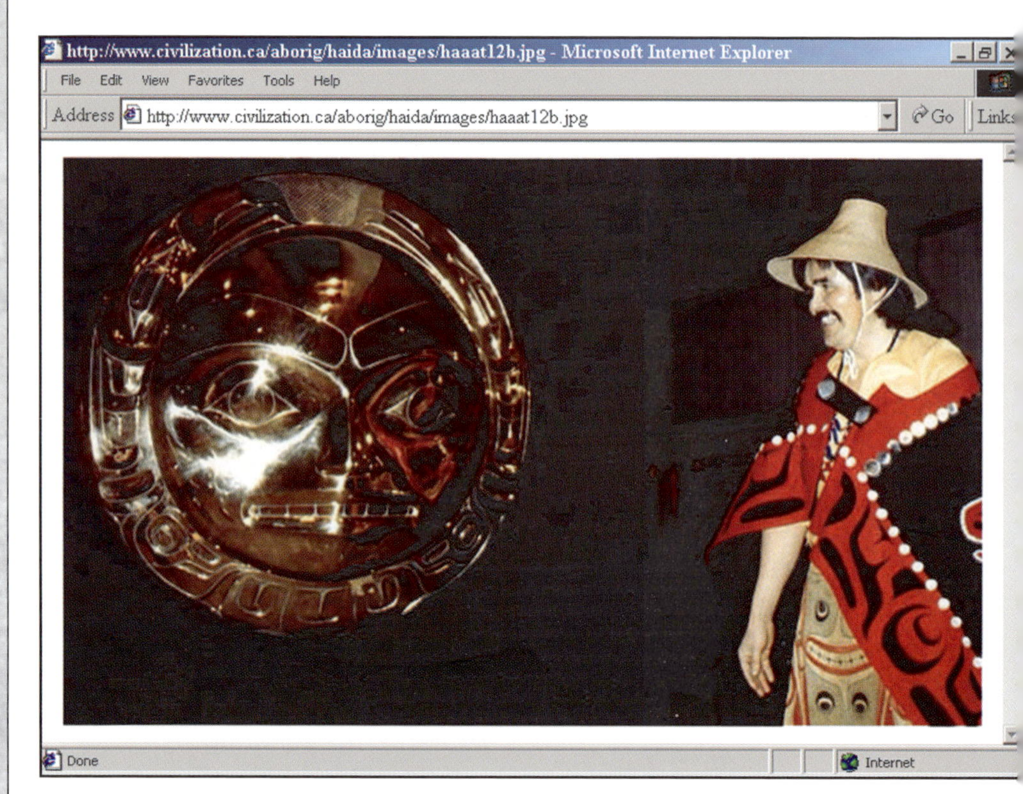

Haida sculptor Robert Davidson stands by Raven Bringing Light to the World, *one of his works of art.*

a million acres in Manitoba, but the federal government still controlled all the natural resources. But fewer than a thousand Métis were able to keep the title to the land they were granted.

The French

French-speaking people make up almost one fourth of the population of Canada. Most of them live in Quebec. There have been political movements that tried to separate Quebec from the rest of Canada, but those movements have been voted down, although the French influence throughout the country is seen in products produced in Canada which carry labels in both English and French. Montreal and Quebec City are both dominated by French-Canadian culture and the French language.

Canadian Art and Architecture

Canadians have distinguished themselves in the fine arts. One of the earliest Canadian painters was Cornelius Krieghoff, who painted scenes of Quebec. Paul Kane was another early artist who specialized in painting North American Indians and their way of life.

The most influential painters in Canada were known as the Group of Seven. Lawren S. Harris, J.E.H. MacDonald, Arthur Lismer, Frederick Varley, Frank Johnston, Franklin Carmichael, and A.Y. Jackson were landscape painters who put on their first exhibition in 1920.

Canada's leading modern painters include Alexander Colville, Jack Shadbolt, Toni Onley, and Gordon Smith. Robert Murray and David Rabinovitch are important Canadian sculptors. Robert Davidson is a well-known Haida (Indian) sculptor.

Canadian architecture has been influenced by many earlier styles of architecture. Arthur Erickson is one of the most important contemporary Canadian architects. His designs include the Waterfall Building and Robson Square, a three-block-long government complex in Vancouver.

Other notable examples of Canadian architecture include the curved buildings of Toronto's City Hall, the SkyDome where the Toronto Blue Jays play, the National Gallery of Canada in Ottawa, and the CN Tower in Toronto.

Music, Dance, and Theater

Most major cities in Canada have symphony orchestras. The first was founded in Quebec in 1902. Well-known

instrumental musicians from Canada include pianists Oscar Peterson and Glenn Gould, classical guitarist Liona Boyd, and saxophone player Jane Bunnett. The Canadian Opera Company tours the country.

Canada has three top-ranking ballet companies: The National Ballet Company of Canada, the Royal Winnipeg Ballet, and the Grands Ballets Canadiens. Children attend Toronto's National Ballet School in hopes of becoming great ballet dancers. Modern dance is also popular in Canada.

Folk dancing is popular as well. The many immigrant groups who have settled in Canada have helped keep their traditions alive by performing folk dances from their countries.

Theater has flourished in Canada since World War II. Stratford, Ontario, is home to the Stratford Festival of Canada, which is the largest classical repertory theater in North America. It features the works of William Shakespeare and Greek dramatists as well as modern playwrights. George Bernard Shaw's plays are featured at the Shaw Festival in Niagara-on-the-Lake, Ontario.

Sports

Ice hockey originated in Canada and is still a very popular sport. Canada also has two major league baseball teams, the Montreal Expos and the Toronto Blue Jays, as well as a professional basketball team, the Toronto Raptors, part of the National Basketball Association. Canadian football, which differs from American football in several ways, is also popular.

Chapter 4

Economy

The economy of Canada is similar to that of the United States: Both countries are affluent and have high-tech industrial societies. Standards of living are high in both countries. In the past fifty years, Canada's economy has changed from a mostly rural economy to an economy that is primarily industrial and urban.[1]

Canada's major products include minerals, food products, wood and paper products, transportation equipment, chemicals, fish products, petroleum, and natural gas. Canada's major industries are agriculture, fishing and trapping, forestry and logging, energy, and mining.

Canada's largest trading partner, by far, is its neighbor to the south. About 85 percent of Canada's exports are sold to the United States. This relationship is not always to Canada's benefit, however. Because the two countries' economies are so connected, Canada follows the United States when its economy is in decline.[2]

Agriculture and Fishing

Major crops grown in Canada are spring wheat, barley, alfalfa, canola, and other hay and fodder crops, which are fed to livestock. Most grain is raised in the Prairie Provinces of Manitoba, Saskatchewan, and Alberta.

Fruits and vegetables are also raised in Canada, mainly in Ontario, Quebec, and British Columbia. Fruits include blueberries, apples, and grapes. The major vegetables raised in Canada are sweet corn, peas, and green or wax beans.

Cattle, sheep, pigs, and poultry are the main types of livestock that Canadians raise. Most dairy farms are in Quebec, Ontario, and Nova Scotia while most beef cattle are raised in Alberta and Ontario.

Canada is the world's leading exporter of fish. Cod and herring are the leading fish exports, followed by halibut, redfish, and turbot. Canada also exports shellfish. These include clams, scallops, oysters, shrimp, and crabs.

Forestry and Logging

Since more than 40 percent of Canada's land is forested, lumbering has always been an important industry. However, forests have been overcut, and a program of reforestation (replanting where trees have been cut) has been started. Besides lumber, forests provide pulp for

A famous event, the Calgary Stampede, features a famous group of Canadians: the Royal Canadian Mounted Police, also known as Mounties.

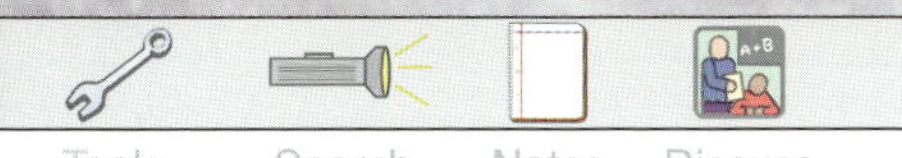

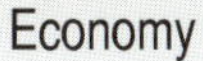

making paper. Canada exports both the pulp and newsprint (paper for newspapers) made from trees.

Energy and Mining

Canada's many rivers provide hydroelectric power. Their resources also include large amounts of oil and natural gas, which can be used for energy.

Under Canadian soil is a wealth of valuable minerals. Besides the fuels mentioned, Canada has large deposits of coal, iron ore, and nickel. The country is the leading exporter of uranium and ranks third in exports of zinc.

Manufacturing and Services

Since World War II, Canada's manufacturing has increased greatly. Motor vehicles are the most important product, but high-tech products and products in the computer and space industries have become increasingly important.

Many Canadians are employed in providing services. These include workers in banks, the insurance business, stores, health, and schools. Tourism is also an important industry in Canada.

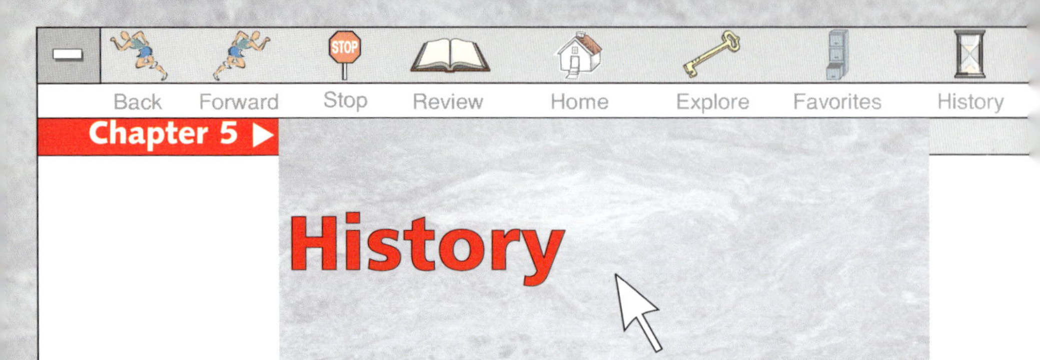

Chapter 5

History

Thousands of years before the first Europeans reached North America, native people from Asia crossed what was then a land bridge into Canada. By the time Columbus arrived in the New World in 1492, these people had spread throughout Canada.

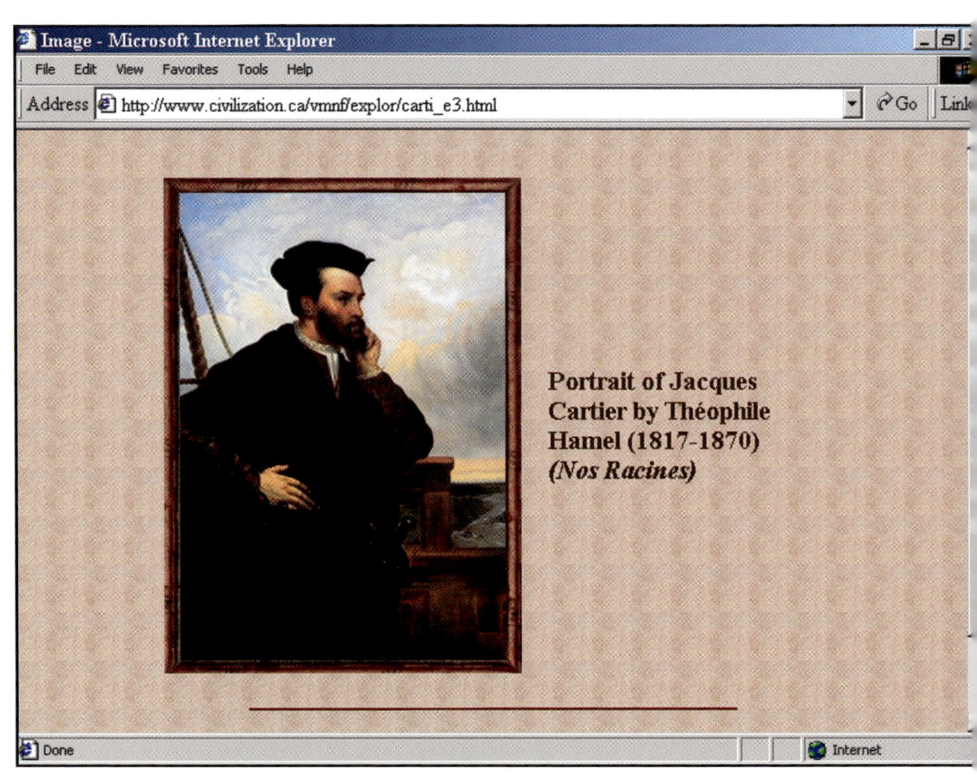

French navigator and explorer Jacques Cartier explored the St. Lawrence River region for France, although his aim, which had been to find a Northwest Passage to Asia, was never achieved.

About A.D. 1000, a group of Viking farmers and craftspeople established the first European settlement in North America in what is today the northernmost part of Newfoundland. The settlement lasted only a short time, however. It is believed the Norse settlers were forced out by the area's aboriginal people.[1]

French and British Settlement

The French were the first Europeans to stake a claim in what is now Canada. Jacques Cartier claimed the area around the St. Lawrence River in 1534. French trappers began moving into the area and established trading posts. France paid little attention to its new colony, New France, in the 1500s.

Samuel de Champlain explored the St. Lawrence River area for the French in the early 1600s. In 1608, he founded the city of Quebec in the heart of New France. Montreal was established in 1642 as a missionary outpost.

In 1663, New France officially became a province of France. By then, there were about sixty thousand French settlers in Canada.

In 1670, England founded the Hudson's Bay Company and began trapping in the area of Hudson Bay. They based their claims on the explorations of John Cabot, an Italian who had sailed for England and first sailed along Canada's eastern shore in 1497.

The French and Indian Wars

Conflict arose between French and British claims in Canada. France and Great Britain were involved in a series of wars from the late 1600s to the mid-1700s that have come to be known as the French and Indian Wars. These wars pitted not only the colonial powers against one

The French fortress at Louisbourg, in Acadia (now Nova Scotia), guarded the entrance to the St. Lawrence River.

another but also divided aboriginal people into alliances. In 1710, the British captured Port Royal, in Acadia (now Nova Scotia), the first permanent European settlement in Canada. A 1713 treaty also made France surrender other territories around Hudson Bay, Newfoundland, and Acadia to the British.

France then founded the powerful Fortress of Louisbourg on Cape Breton Island, Nova Scotia, to protect the entrance to the St. Lawrence River. It became the most highly fortified fort in North America.

In 1745, an army of New Englanders attacked Louisbourg, Nova Scotia, with ninety ships and four thousand men. Men from the fort had been preying on American merchant ships. Louisboug was forced to surrender, but was returned to France by a treaty in 1748.

By 1756, France and Great Britain were also fighting a war in Europe, known as the Seven Years' War. The wars in the American and Canadian colonies had broken out because of rivalry over the fur trade and the Ohio River Valley. Fighting began in the Ohio Valley in 1754. France scored early victories at Fort Oswego and Fort William Henry. But in 1758, the French lost the great fort of Louisbourg.

The next year, the British stormed and captured Quebec. French military commander Marquis de Montcalm de Saint-Véran was killed, and the French were defeated. In 1760, the French surrendered Montreal to the British.

When the Treaty of Paris was signed in 1763, France ceded all its North American possessions east of the Mississippi River, including Canada, to Great Britain.

Canada's Growth

The Quebec Act of 1774, however, extended Quebec's borders west and south, which infuriated American colonists. In fact, the first act of the American Continental Congress was not to declare independence from Great Britain but to invade Canada and persuade its citizens to join the American fight against the British. That invasion, known as the Quebec Campaign, did not succeed, however. During the remainder of the American Revolution, between 1775 and 1783, Canada's population grew quickly. About fifty thousand loyalists moved from the United States to Canada so they could remain under British rule.[2] Many British loyalists from America settled

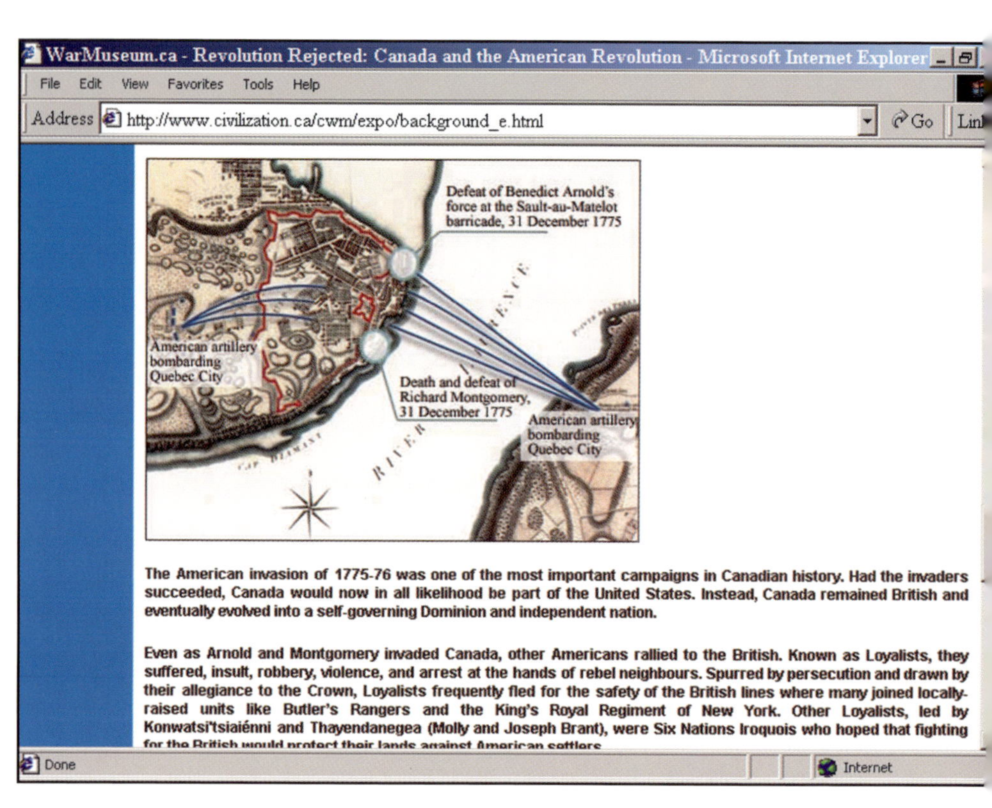

The American invasion of 1775-76 was one of the most important campaigns in Canadian history. Had the invaders succeeded, Canada would now in all likelihood be part of the United States. Instead, Canada remained British and eventually evolved into a self-governing Dominion and independent nation.

Even as Arnold and Montgomery invaded Canada, other Americans rallied to the British. Known as Loyalists, they suffered, insult, robbery, violence, and arrest at the hands of rebel neighbours. Spurred by persecution and drawn by their allegiance to the Crown, Loyalists frequently fled for the safety of the British lines where many joined locally-raised units like Butler's Rangers and the King's Royal Regiment of New York. Other Loyalists, led by Konwatsi'tsiaiénni and Thayendanegea (Molly and Joseph Brant), were Six Nations Iroquois who hoped that fighting for the British would protect their lands against American settlers.

American colonists hoped to convince their Canadian counterparts to join them in their revolution against the British. Had the American invasion of Quebec in 1775 and 1776 succeeded, it is likely that the British colonies in northern North America would have become part of the United States—and Canada as a dominion would never have come into being.

in Nova Scotia, while others settled on the western edge of Quebec, spilling over into what is now Ontario.

This migration to Canada was important, because now the English-speaking settlers outnumbered the French-speaking settlers. In 1784, part of Nova Scotia, which had been predominantly French, was carved out to form New Brunswick for these English-speaking settlers. Quebec and Ontario soon grew large enough to have their own governors.

War of 1812

In 1812, war broke out again between Great Britain and the United States. The immediate cause of the war was British insistence on searching American ships for deserters from their own navy. The Americans also felt the British settlers in Canada were inciting the Indians to attack their settlements near the Canadian border.

A number of battles were fought along the border, but the United States was unsuccessful in its attacks. The outcome of the war permanently established by 1818 the present boundary between the United States and Canada.

Government of Canada

In 1791, Canada had been divided into two sections. Upper Canada was mostly British, and Lower Canada was French. In 1841, the Act of Union brought them together as United Canada, but disagreements over representation continued for more than twenty years.

Sir John A. Macdonald was instrumental in Canada's confederation as a dominion. He was elected Canada's first prime minister in 1857.

The Dominion of Canada Is Established

In 1864, representatives of United Canada (formerly Upper and Lower Canada) and the Maritime colonies met at Charlottetown, in Prince Edward Island. John Macdonald and George-Étienne Cartier proposed uniting all the colonies under one national government. Macdonald had served as joint premier of Canada, and Cartier had participated in the earlier rebellions. George Brown, owner of the Toronto newspaper the *Globe*, explained how the government would work.

By the end of the conference, most representatives were convinced that confederation would work. The delegates then met in Quebec, where they settled on a federal system in which each province would have its own legislature and in which powers would be divided between the federal and provincial governments.

The next step in Canada's self-government was the London Conference, or Westminster Conference, in 1866 and 1867. John Macdonald chaired this conference, where a plan of confederation was worked out. The British North America Act of 1867 formally established the Dominion of Canada. (In 1982, this act was renamed the Constitution Act, 1867.)

Ontario, Quebec, New Brunswick, and Nova Scotia were the first four provinces. Other areas would be included in the Dominion as their populations grew. John Macdonald served as Canada's first prime minister. He believed in a strong, centralized form of government.

Canada Expands Westward

In 1868, the British decided to transfer their lands in the west to Canada. Most of the people in the area lived along

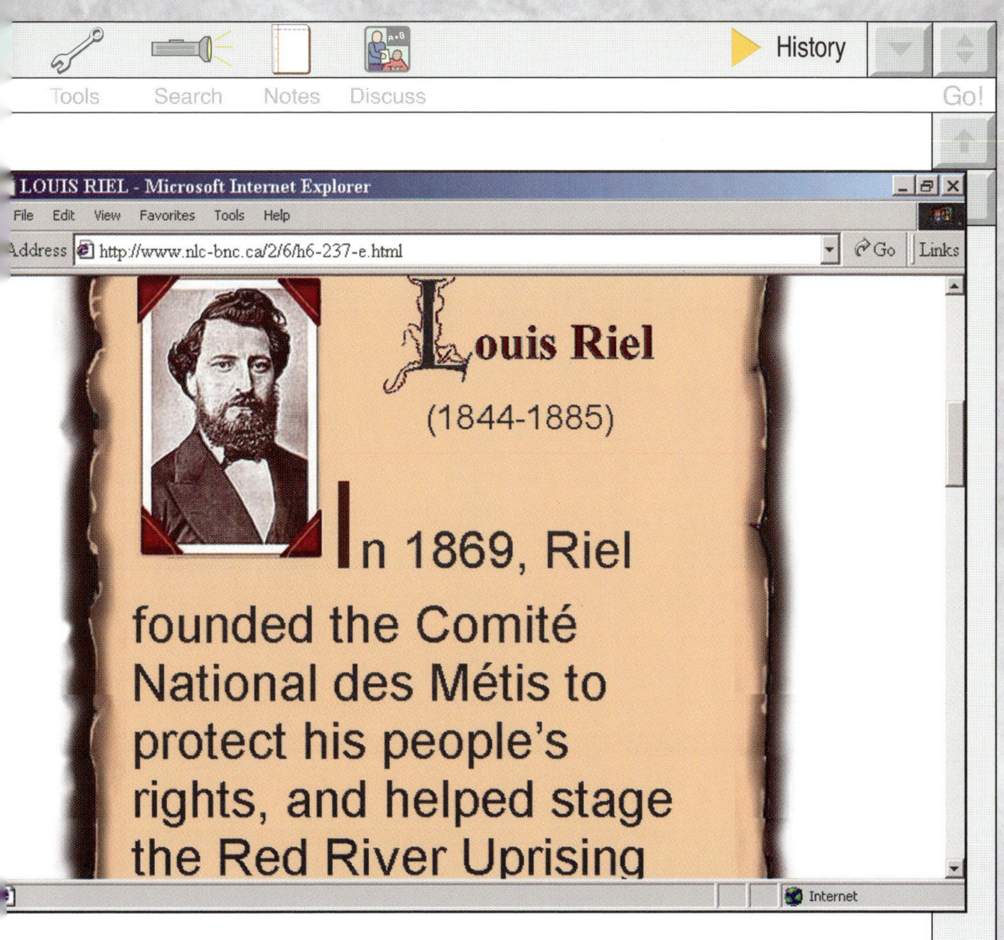

Louis Riel was an early leader of the Métis people in western Canada.

the Red River, in what is now Manitoba, and over ten thousand of them were Métis. They felt threatened because the British were giving their land away with no input from them.

Louis Riel became their leader and in 1869 and 1870, he and others staged two rebellions against the Canadian government. In the Red River rebellion, Riel's men seized Fort Garry and established a Métis government there. In 1870, the Manitoba Act made Manitoba the fifth province of Canada, and Riel was elected to the House of Commons. But he was expelled in 1874 and banished the next year. He returned in 1884 to lead another rebellion,

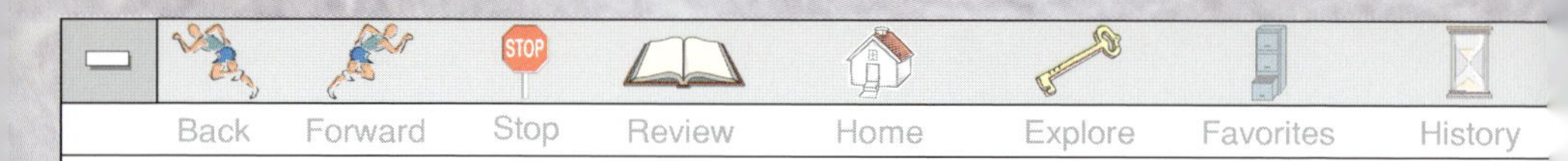

this one in Saskatchewan, but he was captured, tried for treason, and hanged. During the next few years, Alberta, British Columbia, and the Northwest Territories gained more settlers along the West Coast of Canada.

Canada's east and west coasts were finally linked together when the Canadian Pacific Railway was completed in November 1885. By 1905, all the provinces but Newfoundland and Labrador were part of the Canadian federation. That province became Canada's tenth province in 1949.

Canada grew immensely in population from the end of the nineteenth century to the beginning of the twentieth. In the years between 1891 and 1914, 3 million immigrants,

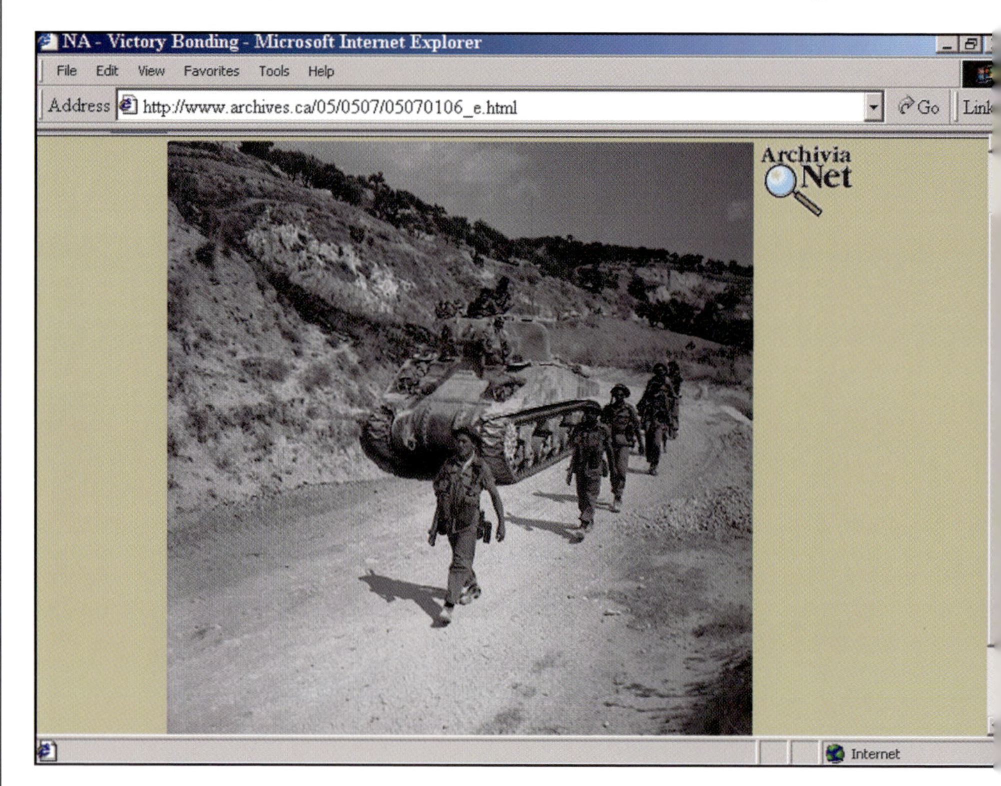

Canada in World War II: Members of Princess Patricia's Canadian Light Infantry are photographed advancing past a tank in Italy in July 1943.

mostly from Europe, settled in Canada, following the path of the new transcontinental railway.

Influence of the World Wars

Canada's influence and prosperity grew steadily after World War I, which lasted from 1914 until 1918. Canada fought on the side of the Allies, with England, France, and eventually, the United States. In 1931, the Statute of Westminster made Canada a voluntary member of the British Commonwealth of Nations, still an independent country but also still linked to Great Britain.

During World War II, from 1939 to 1945, Canadians again fought alongside the British and Americans. Now they entered into defense agreements with the United States on their own, though. Canada emerged from the war with a greater standing in the world and joined NATO (the North Atlantic Treaty Organization) in 1949.

After World War II, Canada experienced another huge increase in population. Many immigrants arrived from Europe, the economy was good, and trade and manufacturing grew.

In 1959, the St. Lawrence Seaway opened, linking the five Great Lakes with the St. Lawrence River. This made it possible for goods to be shipped from ports on any of the lakes all the way to the Atlantic.

More Immigrants

The 1960s brought a new wave of immigrants from Asia, the Caribbean, and Central and South America. In 1967, Canada celebrated its one hundredth anniversary by hosting the World's Fair in Montreal. It was called Expo 67.

In 1992, Canada signed the North American Free Trade Agreement (NAFTA) with the United States and

Captured on Parliament Hill in Ottawa is the colorful pageantry of the Ceremonial Guard of the Canadian Forces.

Mexico, and it took effect in 1994. In 1999, Nunavit was added as a third territory, carved from the Northwest Territories. Its inhabitants are mostly Inuit.

The French in Quebec

Since the 1970s, there has been a movement in Quebec to separate from the rest of the country. Many of the French-speaking citizens of Quebec want to be recognized as a distinct society with special rights.

In 1976, the political party that wanted Quebec to leave the Dominion won the election in Quebec. However, in 1980 a vote found that 60 percent of the people of Quebec were against independence. In 1982, a Charter of Rights and Freedoms for Canadians was drawn up. The people of Quebec never approved it, but it passed anyway.

Canadian political leaders have tried to appease the French-Canadian population, especially those in Quebec. French was recognized as one of two official languages in Canada, and government officials have tried to increase the number of public service jobs filled by French-speaking citizens. In 1995, Quebec voters rejected independence, but the referendum was only defeated by a small margin.

Canada Today

Canada was affected by the September 11, 2001, terrorist attacks in the United States, even though those attacks did not take place on Canadian soil. All planes due to land in the United States after the attacks were diverted to Canadian airports when American airports closed down. Canadians fed and housed all the passengers of those planes. Later, in Ottawa, one hundred thousand Canadians gathered on Parliament Hill to honor the victims of 9/11, the largest gathering ever known there.

From its beginnings as a British and French territory, Canada has evolved into a world power, with a diverse and literate people, and a climate of tolerance that is respected throughout the world.

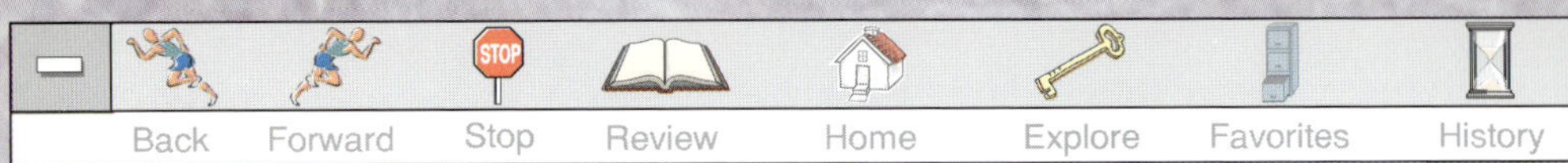

Chapter 6

Canadian Americans

During each year of the 1990s, between twenty-two thousand and thirty-five thousand Canadians immigrated to the United States. Emigration from Canada to the United States increased steadily during those years. The 2000 U.S. census showed that 678,000 people living in the United States claimed Canada as their birthplace.[1]

Educated Immigrants

Some Canadians are concerned about what they call the "brain drain."[2] That is how they refer to the fact that so many well-educated people move from Canada to the United States. They are especially concerned because Canada spent the money to educate these people.

Others have decided the "brain drain" is not nearly as bad as first thought. This is because Canada also gets many immigrants from other countries, and many of them are also well-educated.[3]

Why Canadians Move to the United States

There are several reasons why Canadians move to the United States. Some come because they are able to get better jobs that pay more money. Taxes are also higher in Canada than in the United States, and some immigrants want to escape the high taxes. Not all Canadians leave Canada for financial reasons, though. Many move south for a more temperate climate.

Even though Canadians who immigrate to the United States experience less culture shock than other immigrants, they do miss certain things about their home. Many miss traditional Canadian foods, such as French fries with gravy, a certain kind of orange called Christmas orange, and some kinds of candy. They miss their family and friends back home, too.

How Canadians Here Keep Their Culture Alive

Canadian immigrants enjoy getting together with other people from Canada who live in the United States. They like to talk about home and the things they miss. They try to keep their culture and customs alive in their new country.

There are also Canadian-American clubs throughout the United States. Some, like the Bay Area Canadians in the San Francisco area, are new. Others, like the Canadian Club of Boston, have been around for more than one hundred years. Several message boards have been set up on the Internet for Canadians living in the United States. Participants can talk to other Canadian immigrants about the adjustments they are making.

Canadian Americans, like other immigrants, diversify American culture. Their contributions in the fields of science, art, and entertainment add to the American way of life.

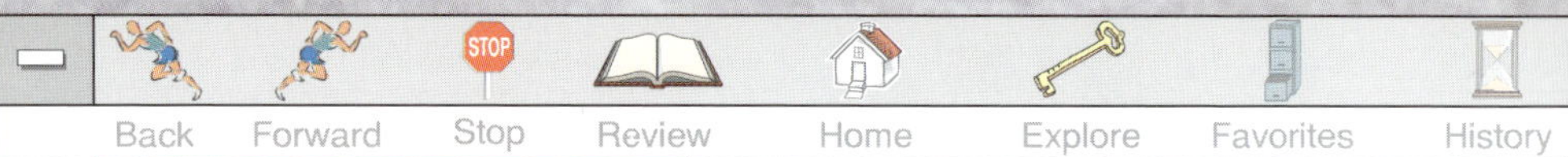

Chapter 1. Canada: Land of Beauty and Resources

1. Andrew H. Malcolm, *The Canadians* (New York: Times Books, 1985), p. 165.

Chapter 2. Land and Climate

1. "Great Lakes/St. Lawrence Lowland," *Get2knowcanada.ca*, n.d., <http://www.get2knowcanada.ca/region_great_lakes.htm> (September 23, 2003).

Chapter 3. Culture

1. "Aboriginal Peoples of Canada: A Demographic Profile," *Statistics Canada*, n.d., <http://www12.statcan.ca/english/census01/products/analytic/companionlabor/contents.cfm?> (September 23, 2003).
2. "Inuit Information Sheet," *Indian and Northern Affairs Canada*, March 2000, <http://www.ainc-inac.gc.ca/pr/info/info114_e.html> (September 23, 2003).
3. Ibid.

Chapter 4. Economy

1. "Canada," *The World Factbook 2003*, n.d., <http://www.cia.gov/cia/publications/factbook/geos/ca.html> (September 23, 2003).
2. Wayne C. Thompson, *Canada 2002* (Harpers Ferry, Va.: Stryker-Post Publications, 2002), p. 137.

Chapter 5. History

1. "The Vikings in Vinland," *Athena Review*, vol. 1, no. 3, n.d., <http://www.athenapub.com/vinland1.htm> (September 2003).
2. Mark Lightbody and others, *Canada* (Oakland: Lonely Planet Publications, 2002), p. 17.

Chapter 6. Canadian Americans

1. *Profile of the Foreign-Born Population of the United States, 2000*, U.S. Census Bureau, 2001, Table 5-2A.
2. "Brain Drain to South of the Border," n.d., <http://www.geocities.com/worldissues2001/brain_drain_first.html> (September 23, 2003).
3. "Brain Drain and Brain Gain," *Statistics Canada—The Daily*, May 24, 2000, <http://www.statcan.ca/Daily/English/000524/d000524a.htm> (September 23, 2003).

Further Reading

Archbold, Rick. *Canada: Our History: An Album Through Time.* Toronto: Doubleday Canada, 2000.

Baldwin, Douglas. *Rebellion and Union in the Canadas.* New York: Weigl Educational Publishers, Ltd., 2003.

Corriveau, Danielle. *The Inuit of Canada.* Minneapolis: Lerner Publishing Group, 2001.

Hehner, Barbara, ed. *The Spirit of Canada.* Toronto: Malcolm Lester Books, 1999.

Jamieson, Marshall. *Beginnings: From the First Nations to the Great Migration.* Edmonton: Reidmore Books, 1996.

Kalman, Bobbie. *Canada: The People.* St. Catharines, Ont., Canada: Crabtree Publishing Company, 2002.

Kissock, Heather. *Canada Day.* New York: Weigl Educational Publishers, Ltd., 2003.

Nickles, Greg, and Niki Walker. *Canada.* Austin, Tex.: Raintree Publishers, 2000.

Owens, Ann-Maureen, and Jane Yealland. *Forts of Canada.* Toronto: Kids Can Press, 1996.

Yee, Paul. *Struggle and Hope: The Story of Chinese Canadians.* Toronto: Umbrella Press, 1996.

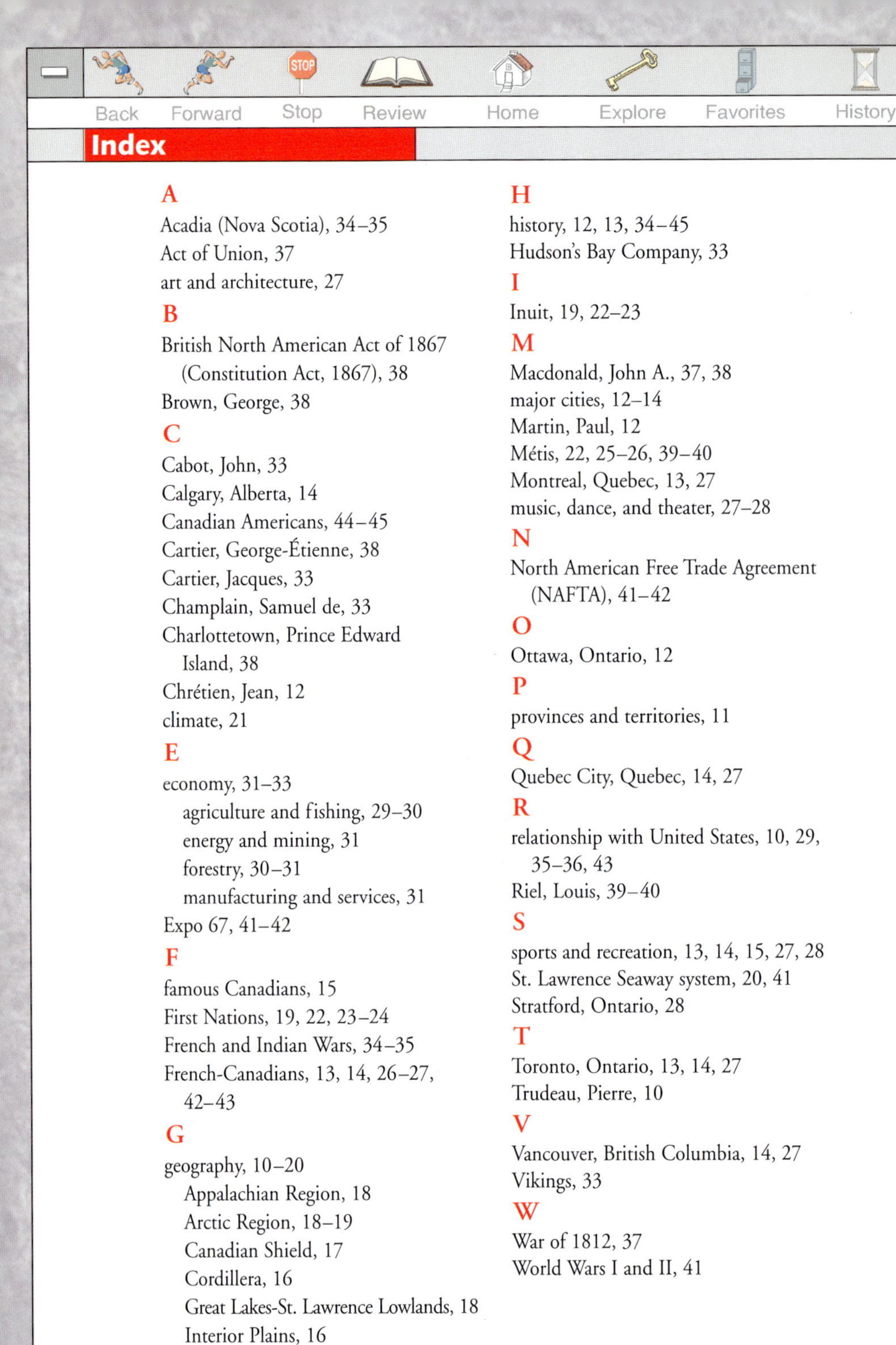

Back
Forward
STOP
Stop
Review
Home
Explore
Favorites
History

Index